W9-AMB-064

To:

_____

From:

_____

When I wrote this story in 1977, I wanted to explore a father-and-son bonding experience from the child's perspective. And perspective is key here, because Little Critter doesn't interpret things the way a parent (or an objective reader) might. Although he has the best intentions, things don't always go as planned . . . and that's okay. We can see from the way he tells the story that their (mis)adventure has meant a great deal to him.

I love experimenting with the humor that comes from the divergence between pictures and words—between what really happens and how it's perceived through the lens of a child's imagination. My hope is that through laughter and learning, this book and every other Little Critter book will help create new bonding experiences between parent and child.

—Mercer Mayer

"The world is a very strange and mysterious place, full of anything possible. To a child, their imagination is reality. To them, whatever they imagine could be real. Learning to deal with things in life—friends, pets, monsters, camping, whatever . . . is a challenging thing."
—Mercer Mayer

Just Me and My Dad book, characters, text, and images copyright © 1977, 2021 by Mercer Mayer. Little Critter, Mercer Mayer's Little Critter, and Mercer Mayer's Little Critter and Logo are registered trademarks of Orchard House Licensing Company. All rights reserved. Published in the United States by Random House Children's Books, a division of Penguin Random House LLC, 1745 Broadway, New York, NY 10019, and in Canada by Penguin Random House Canada Limited, Toronto. Originally published by Golden Books, an imprint of Random House Children's Books, New York, in 1977. Random House and the colophon are registered trademarks of Penguin Random House LLC.

Visit us on the Web!
rhcbooks.com
littlecritter.com

Educators and librarians, for a variety of teaching tools, visit us at RHTeachersLibrarians.com

ISBN 978-0-593-37624-9 (hardcover)

MANUFACTURED IN CHINA

10 9 8 7 6 5 4 3 2

Random House Children's Books supports the First Amendment and celebrates the right to read.

Penguin Random House LLC supports copyright. Copyright fuels creativity, encourages diverse voices, promotes free speech, and creates a vibrant culture. Thank you for buying an authorized edition of this book and for complying with copyright laws by not reproducing, scanning, or distributing any part in any form without permission. You are supporting writers and allowing Penguin Random House to publish books for every reader.

JUST ME AND MY DAD

BY MERCER MAYER

Random House 🏠 New York

We went camping,
just me and my dad.
Dad drove the car
because I'm too little.

I picked the campsite, but someone
was already living there.
So I gave it back.

We found another
campsite nearby.
My dad was tired,
so I pitched the tent.

We made a campfire.
I found the wood,
and my dad lit the fire.

I wanted to take my dad
for a ride in our canoe,
but I launched it too hard.

We went fishing instead.

My dad took a snapshot
of the fish we caught.
Then I cooked dinner
for me and my dad.

We had eggs.

After dinner, I told my dad a ghost story.
Boy, did he get scared!

I gave my dad a big hug.
That made him feel better.

Then we went to bed.

I stayed up with my dad and let him read a story to me.

We slept in our tent all night long—
just me and my dad.

Wait, there's more!

Turn the page to look at never-before-seen
sketches by Mercer Mayer, the author and
illustrator of Little Critter!

A LOOK BEHIND THE BOOK!

Like most illustrators, Mercer Mayer starts the artwork for each book with a rough sketch of every page, plus the cover. This way, he can figure out where to put the characters and leave space for the words.

Illustrators also add background details in the sketch stage. Background details help the reader figure out where the characters are and what is happening.

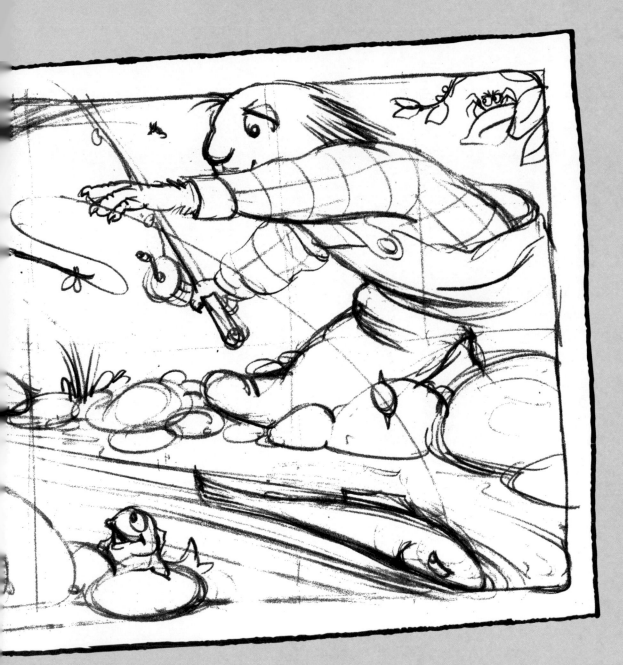